MYSTERIOUS MONSTERS

BOOK 5:
WEREWOLF

COMING TO A BASEMENT NEAR YOU

Mysterious Monsters: Werewolf

For more information, to inquire about rights to this or other works, or to purchase copies for special educational, business, or sales promotional uses please write to:

Corgi bits

Corgi Bits is an imprint of Incorgnito Publishing Press
A division of Market Management Group, LLC
300 E. Bellevue Drive, Suite 208
Pasadena, California 91101

FIRST EDITION

Printed in the United States of America

ISBN: 978-1-944589-35-6

10 9 8 7 6 5 4 3 2 1

For Adam and Susan

Contents

PREFACE

WEREWOLF!

Dear Readers,

I am of two minds about warning you not to read this book. After all, you are holding the *fifth* account of the Mattigan kids' adventures in your hands. And if you've already braved the first four, then I'm quite certain there's nothing I can possibly say to make you put this new one down.

You already know that Maddie (12), Max (10), and Theo (8) are hiding an alien, a vampire, a Sasquatch, and now something like a ghost in the basement of their creaky mansion at the edge of Portland's Forest Park. You also know the kids are not only hiding them from the world, but from their own father, since he happens to be in the business of proving that beings like them don't exist.

And you're good with all that.

So, I bet if I said, "This book *also* has a creature in it that, on certain nights, turns into a vicious beast who'd love nothing more than to rip your face off — and eat it," you'd probably say, *Wow, sounds fascinating. Tell me more.*

Well, there *is* more: This book has more than one new mysterious monster in it!

The first, as you have surely guessed, is a real-life, howling-at-the-moon Werewolf. Which should be scary enough. The second is a creature most people consider the very picture of beauty and charm. But, trust me, you would not want to meet an angry one. Even if you eat people's ripped-off faces.

There's even a third new monster in this book, although, if a certain "news" magazine is to be believed, it won't bother you if you don't stick your hand into its crib.

I can hear you saying, *Great, let's do this.*

See, I know this about you now. *You,* I think, are almost as unusual as the Mattigan kids. I think you're a bit of a monster-hunter yourself.

So, go ahead, read the book. Maybe it's just the kind of thing you've been searching for.

Is it possible that searching is contagious?

Discuss among yourselves.

I ask because it turns out that the very same mysterious monsters who our plucky Mattigans have been searching for are searching for something themselves.

What are *you* searching for, by the way — other than a good book?

Could it be that we are all searching for the same thing?

Let's check in at the end to compare notes, shall we?

I just hope we can face whatever we find along the way (and that we still have faces left after we face it).

CHAPTER ONE

THE MBI

"Greetings! I'd like to officially call to order the first meeting of — I guess we don't have a name for our organization, do we? Any suggestions?" J-Rod looked around at the members of his investigative team, who all looked at one another for ideas.

The team consisted of one almond-eyed, no-nosed, slitty-mouthed alien in a sweatsuit (J-Rod); one massive — and massively furry — giant (Bigfoot); one very well-dressed, but also very pale, vampire (Dracula); and one pitch-black, not-a-spirit-of-the-dead ghost (Shade). And, of course, three wild-haired Mattigans, too.

The group had set up shop in their headquarters, which was the seventh room the kids had taken over in their maze of a basement. Which left about a million more, if they needed them. The kids had furnished it as they had the others, with what they could find in their father's oversupply of fixed-up furniture. It was supposed to look like precinct rooms on police shows. They'd dragged in two old desks and a bunch of rolling chairs, and they'd hung up bulletin boards all over the walls to tack evidence on.

So far, the boards were empty.

"Monster Squad!" Theo suggested.

"I think that name's taken," Maddie told him.

"Monsters, Inc.!"

"Taken."

"Monster Cops!"

"Hmmm."

"Taken," Max said, holding up his phone.

"*Humpf* on *thumpf!*"

"Anyway," Max said. "We're not cops. We can't arrest people. We investigate mysteries — more like the FBI."

"How about "The *Monsters* Bureau of Investigation?" J-Rod suggested.

"The *M*BI?" Theo asked.

Everyone looked at one another, pleased.

"Shall we vote?" J-Rod asked.

Feet, fists, and fingers rose into the air.

"It's unanimous," J-Rod declared. "Welcome to the first meeting of the MBI. We have two reports. Why don't we start with yours, Shade? I believe you were looking into the disappearance of the kids' mother."

A dark female shape stood up smoothly from her chair and cleared her throat. The kids all expected her to say that she'd learned nothing. After all, their mom had been missing for two years. So, they could hardly believe their ears when she said, "I'm happy to report that I've learned quite a lot. In fact, I've discovered where Layla Mattigan took her final trip."

"WHAT?" all three Mattigans cried out, leaping to their feet.

"How did you manage that?" Maddie asked. "When

the police, and my dad... when no one's been able to figure out *anything?*"

Shade looked at the kids — or seemed to look at the kids — and said, "Yes, well, as you know, I am able to enter people's bodies for a brief period of time and read their minds. I spent my two weeks jumping in and out of everyone involved in the investigation, as well as many of the people they investigated. Each had information about your mother's case, pieces of it, but no one had *enough* pieces to construct the whole picture. It's like a puzzle, you see. Between them all, I was able to put it together."

"Where — where did she go?" Maddie asked. She could see both her brothers were afraid to ask, as if the answer might somehow hurt to know.

"To Vancouver Island," Shade said, "which is in British Columbia, Canada. It's not too far from here, actually. You can drive there in half a day, though you have to take a ferry to the actual island. Well, *you* would, anyway. I believe she stayed at the Vancouver Island Beach Hotel, but that's where the trail runs cold."

Max, Maddie, and Theo were stunned. None of them knew what to make of this incredible news. After being in the dark for so long about their mother's final days, it felt strange to know something: an actual fact. They all wanted to go and tell their father right away, but of course they did no such thing.

"But," Max said after processing the information, "she went to check on some big discovery that was also going to be a huge surprise for my dad. She was a physicist. Did you learn anything about that?"

"Sorry," Shade admitted. "I've told you all I know."

"Well," J-Rod said, "this is outstanding. Very helpful. Thank you, Shade. I think we should pursue that question as soon as possible. Shall we move on to our next order of business?"

Still stunned, the kids took their seats again.

"Dracula, will you share your report?"

"Glahdly," Dracula said, standing up in his stiff and formal way. "My job vas to learn vy not vone of us *monzters* remembers our parents, which is to zay, vy vee all

14

seem to have zimply found ourselves as children being raised by strangers, or vorse, all alone. I vent back to Tranzylvania to zearch records. I flew around Qvatchy's voods here in ze Great Northvest. I flew into ze zecret government mountain vere you lived, Vrody, and read records of ze crashed ship zey found you in. And I flew to ze city in Norvay that Shady here tells us she remembers firzt."

"Outstanding," J-Rod said. Everyone in the room leaned forward in their refurbished chairs, literally on the edges of their seats, waiting to hear what Dracula had discovered. "What did you find out?"

"Zips," Dracula said. "Zeros. Zilches. I am zorry."

Everyone slumped back into their chairs.

"Well," J-Rod replied, trying to keep his alien chin up, "this may seem like a dead-end, but it's only been two weeks, after all. Let's not expect too much, too soon, from *all* of our investigations."

"But it just can't be a coincidence," Max protested.

"Agreed," J-Rod agreed. "Though it appears we

were all born too long ago for any evidence to—"

"Vat vould help," Dracula put in, "vould be to find a baby monzter. Zen ve might be able to—"

Bigfoot suddenly leapt to his feet with a wild yelp and scrambled out of the room, his paws flailing. He looked almost exactly the way he had when, two weeks earlier, the kids' father had come downstairs and almost found them out. The members of the MBI looked at one another once again, this time wondering what had gotten into their furry friend.

A few moments later, the Sasquatch burst back into the room, his arms overflowing with magazines: all of his favorite trashy tabloids full of gossip and phony news. He tossed them on one of the desks, then began frantically sorting through them. Finally, he seemed to have found the one he was looking for. With another yelp, he rushed it over to J-Rod.

The Chief of the MBI looked at the cover, and then at his team. "Well, how do you like that?" he asked. "Outstanding."

"What?" everyone asked.

J-Rod turned the magazine around. On the cover was a picture of a baby in a crib with razor-sharp teeth and a bit of a fin on its back. The headline read in giant letters: "Orphanage Hiding Vicious Shark-Baby."

"Our dad showed us that one!" Maddie cried out.

J-Rod turned it back around to look closer at the smaller print under the picture. "Well, how do you like *that?*" he asked after reading it.

"*What?*" his team practically begged.

"It seems our two investigations might, in fact, be one." J-Rod looked up at his team with his giant almond eyes. "According to this normally not-worth-the-paper-it's-printed-on magazine," he explained, "the 'vicious shark-baby' was spotted, of all places, in Victoria."

"Where's that?" Max and Maddie both asked.

"On Vancouver Island, British Columbia, Canada."

CHAPTER TWO

PLAN D

"Dad?" Maddie and her brothers had found Marcus Mattigan in his workshop on the first floor. He was sanding down an old table he'd picked up at a garage sale the other day.

The MBI had discussed different options for investigating Vancouver Island before ending their meeting. One idea was to send the monsters there as a group, but that had quickly been dismissed as far too risky. The next suggestion had been to send only Shade and Dracula, since they could travel quickly and hide easily, but it had been decided that, for now, it was best for them to stay hidden, at least while there was a chance the kids could solve the mysteries by themselves. So, Max, Maddie, and Theo had come to tempt their father into one more summer trip.

"What's up?" Marcus asked after setting down his sanding block and taking off his goggles. His overflowing Mattigan hair was stuffed up into a cap to keep it from bothering him while he worked.

"We have an idea for you," Max said.

"It can't be tabled for later?" Marcus asked. "*Tabled* for later. See what I did there?"

His kids just stared at him.

"I guess that one was a little rough around the edges."

"Dad!"

"Okay, okay. Lay it on me."

"Remember this?" Maddie handed her father Bigfoot's tabloid, which the gossip-loving beast had only let her have after she'd promised to bring it right back.

"Of course," Marcus said, shaking his head at the photo of the shark-baby on the cover.

"Great," Maddie said. "Because we think you should—"

"Because it's easily the most ridiculous story of the year."

"But, but—" Maddie sputtered. They hadn't even discussed a Plan B.

"But, look," Max said, holding out his phone. "This says people up there have been bothering the kids at the orphanage since the story came out. So many people have been coming around, trying to get in or to peek through the windows, that the kids were all freaking out. They've had to move them all to a secret location."

"People!" Theo sighed, or sigh-shouted, really.

Max and Maddie flashed him the "good-but-take-it-down-a-notch" look.

"That is disturbing," Marcus allowed. "But it's clear the orphanage wasn't *claiming* to have a shark-baby. And it sounds like the problem was solved."

"Oh, well, right," Max agreed. "But—" Now he was stumped, too.

"Interestingly," Marcus told the kids while they wracked their brains for a new idea, "Vancouver Island is one of the places mermaids have supposedly been sighted over the years."

"*That* would be a great episode for your show!" Maddie cried. "Could we go up and look into that?"

"I'm afraid that idea is all wet," Marcus said. Then he waited.

"*We see what you did there,*" Maddie sighed. "How come?"

Marcus smiled. Then he said, "My producer and I have discussed mermaids a few times. They're a low priority because people don't like to hear that they're not real. Not that I care much about that, but there are always so many other frauds around to expose. Has there been a sighting up there recently?"

"Well, no," Maddie admitted. "Not that we know of."

So much for Plan B.

"Werewolf!" Max suddenly announced. He'd only been half-listening to the mermaid conversation while frantically searching the Web again.

"What?" both his siblings and father asked.

"People saw a werewolf there. *Yesterday!*" Max could

hardly believe their luck. "In the national park," he explained. "I guess the island is pretty foresty. Look!" He handed the phone to his dad, who glanced over the article he'd called up.

"Mermaids, shark-babies, and now a werewolf," Marcus said after handing the phone back. "That island seems to be a vacation hotspot for monsters." He chuckled at the thought. "It is for humans," he added, "so why not? You have some pretty fast fingers, by the way," Marcus added. "Very handy for a spy."

"I see what you did there," Max said. "Not bad."

"*Something's* going on up there," Maddie insisted, trying to stick to the point. "We should go check it out."

"Hmmm," Marcus said.

Max and Maddie exchanged desperate looks. Both were wondering whether they should just tell their father that their mother had disappeared up there. But they knew he wouldn't believe them. And why should he? No, that was a can of worms not worth opening right now.

"One minor detail," Marcus said.

"What's that?" Max and Maddie asked.

"I'm fairly sure imaginary Canadian werewolves are still, you know, *werewolves*."

"What do you mean?"

"The full moon this month isn't until the day after tomorrow."

"Oh."

So much for Plan C, Max and Maddie's looks told each other.

"But the thing is, Dad," Maddie said, having summoned up a Plan D just as the words were coming out of her mouth, "even if this is all a big bunch of balderdash — and I'm sure it is — we'd still really, really like to go."

"We've kinda just been making up excuses with all this monster stuff," Max put in, hoping Maddie had a good idea.

"Oh, really?"

"There's only a few weeks left before school," Maddie explained as the explanation came to her, "and —

24

well, don't get us wrong, we've loved going on all these trips with you, but it's been kind of tiring with all the rushing around. We'd love to do one more, but we want to just sit around working on tans and building sandcastles. We want to go somewhere new and exciting that we've never been to before, but somewhere not too far away."

"Well—"

"Great!" Maddie said. Then, talking fast, she said, "We've taken the liberty of making a reservation starting tomorrow night at the Vancouver Island Beach Hotel. Actually, we made two reservations, because, frankly, I'm done with the whole sleeping on the couch thing. We got adjoining rooms. One for me and Theo, and one for you and Max."

"Now, wait just a minute here!" Marcus objected.

"The hotel," Maddie barreled on, "like the name says, is right on the beach, not too far from where the ferry drops us. We get that at Port Angeles, Washington, which is only four hours away. We're booked on that tomorrow evening, which was the first one we could get tickets for."

"We'll just go pack," Max said.

The kids sprinted for the door.

"Why, you little monsters!"

Max, Maddie, and Theo were already in the hall when their amused, but also outraged, father took a few steps toward the door to demand that they come back right that instant. For that reason, they didn't see him suddenly stop in his tracks. And neither did they hear him whisper, *"Vancouver Island,"* to himself, as if they were the strangest two words he'd ever heard.

CHAPTER THREE

HIDDEN IN ONE PLACE

"So, Dad," Max said the following afternoon as the Mattigan's beat-up old "Yuck" truck rumbled through the Washington countryside, "you ever been to Vancouver Island?"

"Nope," Marcus replied, "but I've always wanted to visit the San Juan Islands. Maybe we can take a ferry around to see them."

"Maybe," Maddie said, looking out the window of her usual front seat spot. Lots of cows. Lots and lots of cows. Then, with her heart pounding, she asked, "How about Mom? Had she ever been up there?"

The kids all held their breath. They knew it would strike their father as very odd for any of them to bring up their mother so randomly, seeing as how they'd pretty much completely stopped talking about her around a year after she'd gone missing. Everyone knew they were always thinking about her, but everyone had somehow silently agreed that talking about her, when no one was looking for her anymore, was just too hard.

But now was the time to take a risk, especially because Marcus was free to talk while they travelled. Since he wasn't expecting to deal with any actual phonies or fraudsters up on Vancouver Island, he didn't need to plan out his investigation while he drove. That gave his kids four hours to get him to spill his guts about their mom's case.

Marcus glanced at Maddie, even though she wasn't looking at him, and then at his boys in the rearview mirror, even though they weren't looking at him, either. "I don't think she ever went up there," he said. "Not to my knowledge, anyway." But then he added, "It's funny you asked, though, because back home, when you guys left to pack, I had a very powerful memory. It's actually why I agreed to go on this trip."

"What memory?" the kids begged. They were look-

ing at him now, all right.

"Is something bothering you guys?"

"We're good," Theo promised.

"What was your memory?" Max asked, turning back to the cows, pretending to be only sort of interested.

"I think, maybe," Marcus said, "it's possible that my father went to Vancouver Island when he abandoned me and my mother."

"WHAT?"

Marcus was so shocked by this outburst that he nearly drove off the road. "Have you guys lost your minds?" he demanded.

"Ha-ha, ho-he-ho!" Theo laughed like a crazy man. "We see what you did there!"

"Um," Marcus said. *What?*

"Tell us what you mean, Dad," Maddie urged, this time giving Theo the "good-but-take-it-down-TEN-notches" look. "We're still feeling bad about believing that imposter who tricked us into thinking he was Grandpa Joe."

29

"Actually, I'm *sure* my father went there," Marcus said. "To Victoria, British Columbia, Canada. I remember because it seemed so far away — like another world." Though his eyes were on the road, they seemed distant. The kids could tell he was getting lost in his thoughts, which led them to share looks of total amazement. Now their grandfather seemed to be involved in this, too! But, they realized at the same time, that actually wasn't so strange after all.

"You guys know he left my mother and me to go in search of cryptids," Marcus continued, "or 'mysterious monsters,' as I've heard you call them. And I think I told you that, even though my mother believed we'd see him again, we never did. She never seemed angry with him, though. I never understood that. I sure was."

"And that's why you hate monsters!" Theo blurted. *"Owwwww!"*

Max had stomped on his brother's foot.

"My bad," Max said, not meaning it.

"Go on, Dad," Maddie urged, giving Theo the worst Eyeballing she'd ever mustered. He was right, of course. But this wasn't the time to bring *that* up.

"You're right, of course," Marcus admitted, though he seemed only barely to have heard the kids. "And I've pretty much admitted to you guys that a big part of my passion for proving how silly it is to believe in those kinds of creatures comes from my anger at him. Aside from the small fact that they actually *aren't* real, of course."

"So, you *still* wouldn't want to know if any mysterious monsters were real?" Maddie asked, unable to help herself.

"*Still* with that question?" Marcus asked. "Why do you keep asking? Are you hiding a bunch of monsters in our basement or something?"

"HA-HA-HA!" Theo roared. "That's a good one, Dad! You're FUNNY! I see what you — *Owwww!*"

"I'm sorry I keep asking," Maddie said. "It's a silly question. You know — *daughters.*"

"Anyway," Marcus said, "the answer to your question is no. I still wouldn't want to know if they were real. I wouldn't even want to think about forgiving my father."

"So," Max said. It was his turn to keep them on track. "You were saying, about Grandpa going to Vancouver Island?"

"Yes," Marcus said, his eyes still on the road, but still a bit dazed. "The day he told us he was leaving, I was ten. I think I told you."

"Max is ten!" Theo announced.

"Go on," Maddie urged.

"Well… you know what I just realized? Just this second?"

"*What?*" all three kids asked, though this time they managed to stifle their screams into a strangled triple-whisper.

"I think that was the day I became a detective, such that I am. See, he told us he was going to "Points Unknown," so when he was talking to my mother after breaking the news, I snuck up to their room and snooped through his luggage. I completely forgot about this until just now. I found a plane ticket. He was actually flying to Victoria, on Vancouver Island. I could see from his passport that he'd flown to Canada many times before, so maybe he'd been going there a lot. I never lifted a finger to find out, or to find him, but from then on, I was interested in exposing liars and making people see that believing in nonsense was a foolish waste of time. I wonder why I forgot that detail until now. Don't get me wrong, kids," he suddenly added, flashing them all quick looks, "I'm not going to spend one minute looking around that island for evidence of my dad having been there. But I am curious what appeal the place might have held for him."

After that, Marcus went silent. His kids went silent, too, but their thoughts were all very much the same. It was clear to them now that all of the mysteries in their lives were connected. The grandfather who'd abandoned their dad, their missing mother and her secret physics work, and the origin of their mysterious monsters — the truth about all of them was hidden in one place.

And soon they'd be there.

CHAPTER FOUR

SILVER BULLETS

The Mattigans travelled on, each lost in his or her own thoughts. Maddie, Max, and Theo were all thinking exactly the same thing, though none of them would have shared the thought, even if they could have, for fear of getting each other's hopes up too high. But they were all thinking it, over and over again, as the Yuck rolled past all those cows: *We are going to find our mother.* They wished they could at least tell their father that his loneliness — all of their loneliness — was finally going to end.

Instead, they said nothing.

The Yuck remained silent the rest of the way.

But that silence was quickly forgotten when the Mattigans arrived at the Port Angeles ferry terminal.

Cars were lined up bumper-to-bumper. Horns were honking. People were shouting out of their windows. Others were on foot, lined up at the ticket windows, complaining. If Maddie hadn't reserved their tickets in advance, there was no way they would've been getting on board that ship.

It took almost an hour, but they got the Yuck in the line for ticketed vehicles and eventually onto the ferry. Then the Mattigans had to fight the crowds trying to get up on deck, which turned out to be standing-room-only. It was so jam-packed that they couldn't get a spot at the rail, so they had to stand in the middle of the crowd. But while they stood there, the kids began to notice a few peculiar things about their fellow passengers.

Maddie made the first observation. "Um," she began, "are girls even allowed on this boat?"

Marcus, Max, and Theo looked at the bodies pressing in all around them. It did seem that nearly everyone was male. But not just male — *extra-large* male. And not just extra-large male: tough-looking, extra-large male.

"There's a lady," Theo said, pointing to a large, rugged-looking woman wedged between two cowboy types, just off to their left.

"Shhh," Max said. "Listen."

So, the Mattigans listened to the loud chattering going on among the men — and at least one lady.

"They're talking about the werewolf," Maddie realized. *"All* of them."

"Um," Max said, looking at his phone again. "I think I know why."

"Something tells me a major sigh is coming on," Marcus said.

"Full moon or no full moon," Max told everyone, "there was another werewolf sighting in that park, or forest, or whatever. Last night."

"So?" Maddie asked. "That hardly explains a boatful of lumberjacks."

"True," Max admitted, "but how about the fact that somebody's offered a reward for its hide? A million bucks!"

"People," Marcus and Theo sighed.

But, for once, Max and Maddie couldn't join the Mattigans' signature sigh. They were too alarmed. And then, in the crush of bodies around them, they both saw one man open his hand to show another man something he'd taken out of his pocket: a bunch of silver bullets.

"Railing!" Theo shouted.

A group had moved away, so the Mattigans swooped into the open spot, relieved to get into the fresh air there, and to be able to see out over the water. Though, in fact, they couldn't see much at all because the ferry was sailing into fog.

Marcus made no further comment about the news. He seemed content just to stand there and look out into the mist with his arm around Theo. After Max exchanged another deeply troubled look with his sister, he took his "spy-nocular" out of his spy kit and peered out over the rail, looking for — he didn't know what. Mermaids, maybe. Maddie turned back to scan the now-even-more threatening collection of passengers on the deck, worried sick that one of them was going to kill the possibly real werewolf. The poor thing needed to come live in their basement if people wanted to shoot it.

Maddie spent the next thirty minutes trying to fig-ure out how she and her brothers were going to deal with a werewolf *and* a shark-baby — not to mention find out what had happened to their mother and what their grandfather had to do with everything. But she couldn't focus after seeing those silver bullets. "Dad," she said, finally giving up, "what are we going to do? All these people — they're going to the island to *kill* the werewolf!"

"This *is* much more serious than I expected it to be," Marcus admitted, turning his attention back from the foggy sea. "I've been thinking — someone could get killed with all these people running around the woods shooting at anything that moves. As far as I know, you can't bring guns into Canada without special permits, or hunt without a guide if you do. But I'm guessing this isn't an especially law-abiding crowd. So, I don't think these rumors are a stunt to lure visitors to the island. But I'll see what I can find out at the office of tourism in the morning."

"I'm sure you'll straighten it out," Maddie said, thinking that, with their dad out of the way, at least they'd be able to look for the shark-baby in peace. She tried to catch Max's eye, to see if he'd realized the same thing, but he was still scanning the fog with his spyglass.

"I may need to recruit a local videographer to come film with me," Marcus said. He turned to Maddie and added, "Werewolves and shark-babies. I guess that's more proof that the island's official department of tourism isn't behind these rumors. If it was, they surely would have mentioned their—"

"Mermaid!" Max suddenly cried out, nearly dropping his spy-nocular. It slid halfway out of his grip, but he managed, barely, to grab hold of the end before it went flying overboard. "I mean," he said, turning around with it again, *"Mermaid.* What you were saying. They surely would have mentioned what they're already known for — their mermaids. The tourism people. Here on the island."

"Right," Marcus said, giving Max a funny look. "Thought you'd seen one there for a second. I was going

to tell you to keep it quiet, because I don't think there are enough boats for the mermaid crowd, too." He smiled at his semi-joke, then turned and looked thoughtfully out into the swirling fog again.

Max went back to scanning the fog with his spyglass. This time, Maddie and Theo exchanged looks… curious ones. Then they stepped in on either side of their brother and leaned in close to him.

"Did you actually see a mermaid?" Theo whispered.

"Pretty sure. She was in the fog, bobbing there, looking at the crowd on the boat."

"What did she look like?"

"She looked — scared."

Maddie understood, but she didn't get the chance to say so, because Theo pointed at the terminal through the suddenly clearing fog and shouted, "Land, ho!"

CHAPTER FIVE

THE ORPHANS

The kids were surprised by Victoria. The cab ride to their hotel took them through wide streets flanked by large buildings no different from those they'd have expected to see in any regular-sized city on the mainland. They'd had no idea the island was so large, or the city of Victoria so… city-like. And the tall, glass-walled Vancouver Island Beach Hotel was, indeed, right on the beach. It sat sandwiched between two other hotels, and there were still more hotels running alongside the ocean in both directions. The whole line of them was surrounded on three sides by lush green forest.

It was past nine when the Mattigans entered the hotel and checked in, so everyone went right to bed.

In the morning, back in Marcus and Max's room

after a light breakfast, everyone discussed their plans for the day.

"Mind if we hang out on the beach?" Maddie asked. All three of the kids were already in their swimsuits.

"Sounds delightful," Marcus said. "I'll walk you out, so we can pick out your home base."

The beach was nearly as crowded as the ferry had been, but it was huge, stretching for what looked like at least a mile in both directions. The day was sunny and clear. Hot, but not too hot. Perfect. The kids chose a spot directly in line with the hotel's front entrance, halfway to the water line, and laid down their towels. It was 10 a.m.

"Now," Marcus said, "You all—"

"Not a foot, not a fist, not a finger!" they all promised.

"Not a sunburn, either."

"Oklahoma," Maddie promised, taking out a spray bottle from the beach bag she'd brought with her. "Sunblock. We're on it."

"Though it works better when it's on you."

"We see what you did there," Max moaned. "Unfortunately."

"Burn," Marcus said, smiling as he headed off. "I'll check in with you around lunchtime."

"What if someone shoots our werewolf?" Theo worried the moment their dad was out of earshot. "Max should have gone with him!"

"I'm concerned about that, too," Maddie admitted. "But there's no way we were going to risk *Max* getting shot."

"Besides," Max said, "our primary mission is finding Mom — I mean, the monster baby. The shark-baby." No one commented on his slip-of-the-tongue, so Max went on, embarrassed to have given away how hopeful he was. "Dad'll tell us what he finds out, anyway," he added. "We'll have to deal with werewolves later. Any ideas how we're going to find Mom? I mean, the shark-baby!"

"Well," Maddie said, "there are only two orphanages on this island. I looked it up. I could just call them and—"

"And what? Ask if they're the ones hiding the shark-baby?"

"Good point."

"And besides," Max pointed out, "the article said the kids were taken to a secret location. I'm pretty sure they didn't take them from one orphanage to hide them in another."

"Another good point."

"They only need somewhere with beds, right?" Max complained. "Maybe a kitchen, too. For all we know, they could be hiding in our hotel, just waiting for all the fuss to blow over."

"Max wins," Theo said.

"So, what are we going to do?" Max demanded.

"I don't know!" Maddie snapped. "What do *you* think we should do?"

"I don't know."

"Theo?" Maddie asked. "Any brilliant ideas?"

"Sure!"

"What?"

"That you guys come up with some brilliant ideas."

"Oh, now *that's* a brilliant idea."

"Told ya."

Stumped, the three Mattigans just sat there, looking at all of the sunbathers lying on towels around them. Hundreds of people were in the water already. Some were on boards of various kinds, though most were just splashing around. There were lots of kids, making lots of noise.

"Well?" Maddie asked after a few minutes of unhelpful silence passed.

"Well, yourself!" Max was feeling unreasonably angry. "I can't think of anything!"

"Me, neither!"

"Okay, try the calls."

Maddie looked up the numbers and made the calls. Not surprisingly, neither of the people who answered admitted to hiding the shark-baby.

"Now what?" Max asked.

"Anything online?"

Max found the original story, but nothing else popped up with it. "Don't see anything new," he said. "Seems like old news now."

"Any ideas now, Theo?" Maddie asked, but he was watching all of the people on the beach, not even trying to help. "Earth to Theo Mattigan!"

"What?"

"Oh, never mind," Maddie sighed. "Let's just think."

All three Mattigans lay down on their towels and thought.

An hour later, they sat up with absolutely no ideas.

"Let's keep thinking," Maddie said.

Another hour passed, and still none of them had a single useful suggestion.

"Let's go eat lunch," Maddie suggested. "I think better on a full stomach."

"Wait a minute," Max said as they gathered up their stuff. He looked at Theo and asked, "Where are your peanut-butter-and-banana sandwiches?"

"Didn't bring 'em."

Max looked at Maddie, who shrugged at him. "So, he didn't bring them," she said, Eyeballing him in a way that meant, *Don't make a big deal about it.*

The kids went back into the hotel and ate lunch in the lobby restaurant. Theo ordered a grilled cheese.

Marcus called while they were eating. He was positive that no one in the government of Vancouver Island had anything to do with the werewolf rumors. They were, in fact, doing everything they could to put a stop to them. They'd closed the park where the sightings had supposedly been made. Shots had already been fired there, but no one had been hurt. And they were planning to film some public service announcements to tell people to go home and forget about the whole thing before someone got seriously injured or killed. Marcus was going to help with those, so he wouldn't be back until probably very late that night, maybe even after ten o'clock.

Which was perfect.

Or it would have been, if they'd had a plan.

Which they didn't.

It was already one o'clock. Max and Maddie were getting frantic.

"Let's go have a nap," Maddie suggested when they were done eating and *still* no ideas had occurred to them. "I always think better after a nap."

Max and Theo protested, but then they agreed to go back up to the rooms. No sooner had they laid down than they, like their sister, fell fast asleep.

Maddie woke them up at four.

"Any ideas?" Max asked.

"No," she admitted. "You?"

"No."

"Let's go back out to the beach. It's freezing in here. I think better when I'm warm."

"But we've already—"

"I know!"

So, they went back out and lay on their towels again.

Another hour passed.

"We've lost the entire day!" Maddie cried. "You're the spy, Max! How would a spy track down a shark-baby hiding out with a bunch of orphans!"

"I don't know, Maddie! Do you think I've been keeping some great idea secret all this time to make things more exciting?"

"Well then, we might as well admit we've failed!" Maddie took out her phone and starting typing on it, hard.

"What are you doing?"

"Texting J-Rod. I'm telling him we totally blew it."

"But, Maddie," Max gasped, "we've never given up before! Mattigans don't do defeat!"

"Well," Maddie shouted, "there's a first time for everything!" She tried to hit *Send*, but before she got the chance, Max grabbed at her phone. He couldn't quite get it away from her, though, and the two of them were suddenly rolling around in the sand, battling for it.

They'd never had anything close to a physical fight before in their entire lives.

"Get off!" Maddie yelled, trying at the same time to tap the phone and get her brother off of her. Finally, she pinned Max to the ground under a knee and ripped the phone away from him.

"Don't send that text!" Max protested.

"Don't tell me what to do!" Maddie felt out of control. Crazy.

"Don't tell me not to tell you what to—"

"Stop! *Where's Theo?*"

CHAPTER SIX

DELPHINE

Maddie let Max up. They both looked around, already worried out of their minds.

"There!" Max said, pointing.

Their brother had wandered off, not far, only about fifteen feet away. He was standing among a group of twenty or so kids sitting on neatly arranged towels. Summer campers, maybe. There were two older teen girls who looked like counselors making sandcastles with some of them. A very tall and very beautiful woman with a baby in one of those little packs on her back was standing at the head of the group. She was talking to Theo.

Who was crying.

Maddie and Max looked at each other, shocked.

Had their fighting upset him that much? Instinctively, they drifted close enough to hear the conversation without calling attention to themselves. They sat down on the sand and pretended to sunbathe.

"Oh, you poor dear!" the woman said to Theo. She had flowing jet-black hair and rosy, red cheeks and long, muscular legs. "Are your parents here on the beach, or staying at one of the hotels?"

"I — I don't know!" Theo wailed. Max and Maddie looked at each other again. Theo was obviously lying to this woman. His lower lip was shaking, just like it did when he melted down for real.

"There, there," the woman said to their brother, patting his shoulder. "Don't worry even one little bit. My name is Delphine. See, I take care of children whose mommies and daddies aren't around. I've been doing this for many, many years, so you can trust me. Say hi, boys and girls."

The kids on the towels, who seemed to range in age from three to eight, all said, "Hi!" and waved at Theo.

This time, Max and Maddie looked at each other, totally stupefied.

"You can stay with us until we find your family," the woman promised. "Would you like that? In fact, this nice hotel right here — and she pointed at the Vancouver Beach Hotel! — has been letting us stay inside for the last few weeks. I know the owner, so they treat us extra special, but tonight's our last night."

"I'm in 1121!" a little girl blurted.

Theo sniffed and nodded, then flashed the tiniest of smiles at his flabbergasted siblings — who hadn't even known he'd seen them watching.

"You can stay with us," Delphine continued, "and I'll help figure out how to locate your parents. We're just going in now to get ready for the big beach costume party. You're welcome to join us, if we haven't found your family first. I'll even help make you a really great cos—"

"What room are *you* in?" Theo sniffled.

"I'm in room 1111. It's big and comfy and—"

"Theo? *Theo!*" Maddie cried, up on her feet and rushing breathlessly to her brother, towel and bag flying behind her. She scooped him up and hugged him like she'd thought she'd never see him again. Max hurried over, pretending to be out of breath, too.

"Oh!" Delphine said to Maddie. "Is this your brother?"

"Yes," Maddie panted. "Thank you so much for taking care of him! He tends to go off on his own. I'm sorry if he was bothering you."

"Not at all! I'm so glad I could help." But then Delphine looked at Maddie curiously and said, "Do I know you?"

"Nope!" Maddie told her. And then she quickly added, "Well, we better be going. Our mother is worried sick. Thanks again!"

And, with that, she took her youngest brother by the hand and the three Mattigans hustled off down the beach.

Back in Maddie and Theo's hotel room, the kids collapsed victoriously on the beds. They'd run straight there.

"How did you know they were orphans?" Max

asked when he caught his breath for real.

"I didn't," Theo said. "Not at first. I just went away from you guys 'cause you were fighting."

"Sorry about that," Maddie said.

"And I heard one of those kids say he hoped they never had to go back to the orphanage. And then I just — made stuff up."

"That was the most incredible thing you've ever done!" Maddie exclaimed. "I swear, it was like you were possessed. Shade isn't in you, is she?"

"Humpf!"

"You would make a great spy," Max said.

"Told ya!"

"No, you didn't."

"Max," Maddie began, checking her phone to confirm that she had actually managed to hit *Send*. She had. "I'm sorry I texted J-Rod. You were right. I gave up too early. I don't know why I lost my head like that. Well, I do. Stress. I do want to solve this mystery. The Mattigan way."

"It's okay," Max said.

"I'll text him back." She tapped out a quick "all good" note.

"Hey," Max said, looking at Theo. "Speaking of stress — where's Mei-mei?"

"At home eating my peanut-butter-and-banana sandwiches with Bigfoot," Theo said. "Why?"

Max opened his mouth, but saw Maddie Eyeballing him big time to let it be. "Anyway—" he said instead, happy to leave the subject behind. He was thrilled that things were finally starting to go their way. Maybe he hadn't been too hopeful. Maybe they *would* actually find their mother. "What's the new plan?" he asked. "Those have to be the right orphans, right? Who is that lady? Does she know what's going on?"

"There's only one way I can think of to find out," Maddie said.

"What's that?" Max and Theo asked.

"We need to break into her room."

CHAPTER SEVEN

MADDIE'S TURN

The kids went down to the main lobby. Since the restaurant was right there, they decided to eat dinner while they waited. At six forty-five, just as they were finishing, Delphine and the orphans came out of the elevator in all sorts of cute costumes. The kids were bunnies and superheroes and police officers and princesses.

Delphine was wearing a long shimmering dress with a tail. She was a mermaid. The baby on her back was a shark.

"I see what she did there," Max said as Delphine led the kids out onto the beach. But then he turned to his brother and sister and said, "I just realized something: the doors here don't use keys. That means I can't pick the locks."

"Wait here," Maddie told him. "Theo, come with me over to the front desk. Time for act two of your show. You're not feeling very well."

"Told ya."

"No, you didn't."

Maddie and Theo walked over to the reception desk.

"Excuse me, sir?" Maddie said to the man standing there.

"Yes?"

"I'm one of the sitters with the—" She looked from side-to-side quickly and added, in a hushed voice, *"orphans."*

"Oh, yes," the man said, his eyes narrowing to show he knew how to keep a secret.

"I'm really sorry, but this one here, little Jimmy, is sick." She stomped on Theo's toe.

"Ow! I mean *Ugh...*" Theo's face got all red and then sort of green. He held his stomach.

"He really doesn't look too good," the man agreed.

"Delphine doesn't want him at the party, but she left her keycard in the room. 1111? Could I trouble you?"

"Sure," the man said. He coded her another card and handed it over.

"Thank you so much."

"No problem."

"When did we become such good liars?" Max asked while the kids waited for the elevator. He hadn't gone on ahead, but rather watched from behind a planter.

"Side effect of searching for mysterious monsters," Maddie said. "And the worst part is, it doesn't even make my stomach hurt anymore."

"That's bad?" Theo asked.

"Yes."

The elevator doors opened and the kids hurried inside. It was one of those glass kinds. So, between that and the hotel's glass walls, they could see right out over the ocean. As they rose up to the eleventh floor, they saw the sun starting to set over the water. The moon was just coming out.

"Well, with the woods closed, at least no one's going to shoot any werewolves," Max said. "One less thing to worry about tonight."

"That's a relief," Maddie agreed.

The elevator came to a stop and the doors opened. "Follow me," Max said. He got into his spy crouch, then started crouching down the thickly carpeted hall. Maddie and Theo looked at each other and rolled their eyes, but they followed him.

Max reached room 1111 first. He pulled a stethoscope out of his spy kit and put it against the door. "All indications are that the room is empty," he declared when his brother and sister arrived. "Gimme the keycard."

Maddie handed it over. Max slipped it into the slot. The latch clicked.

The kids took a quick look up and down the long hall to make sure no one saw them. The coast was clear, so they all bunched up in a clump. Max pushed the door open just a bit, and they pushed into the room, closing the door behind them as quickly as they could.

CHAPTER EIGHT

THE MAN IN THE CHAIR

Just to be on the safe side, Maddie locked the door.

"Uh, Maddie," Max and Theo said at the exact same time and in the exact same disturbed tone of voice.

"What?" she replied, double-checking the door. "That was *way* easier than I thought it would—" Maddie froze mid-sentence, having turned around to see what her brothers were talking about.

The room was *not* empty.

There was a man there, sitting in a chair next to the window. He was thin and pale and had intense eyes and long silver sideburns. But he was not just sitting in the chair.

His arms and legs were tied to it with ropes.

The man's eyes were practically popping out of his skull. He was desperately trying to speak to the kids, but someone had stuffed a washcloth in his mouth. All he could manage were inhuman grunts.

"Oh, my gosh!" Maddie cried. Without thinking, she rushed over and took the washcloth out.

"Thank you! Thank you! Thank you!" the man cried. "I — I was attacked! And then I was tied up and locked in this room!"

"By the orphans?" Max asked, sounding skeptical.

"Orphans?" the man repeated. "I don't know whose room this is! I was walking down the hall when two men attacked me. They hit me and took my wallet and dragged me in here. Please, can you loosen the ropes?"

"Hmmm," Max said. "What if he's the reporter who took the shark-baby picture? What if he tracked them down and Delphine caught him?"

"Shark-baby?" the man scoffed. "That's rubbish! I'm losing feeling in my arms! *Please,* will you help me?"

"Yes, of course we'll help you!" Maddie cried out. She

rushed to loosen the ropes, but the knots were too tight.

"Hold on," Max said. He wasn't sure it was a good idea, but he dug through his spy kit and brought out his Swiss Army knife.

"Brilliant," the man said. "You're one of those types who's prepared for anything, aren't you?"

"I'm a spy," Max explained.

"Very impressive."

"It's what I do." Feeling pride in his profession, Max set to work cutting the ropes.

The moment they were off, the man jumped out of his chair and rushed to the window. He swept the drapes open so wildly that he nearly tore them right off the wall. The sun had set, and though the twilight was anything but dark, the moon was clearly visible.

The gorgeous full moon.

The man let out a terrific howl, which the kids took as a cry of joy at being set free.

That is, until thick tufts of hair started sprouting from the back of his neck.

CHAPTER NINE

THE ATTACK

It happened so fast, and it was so mesmerizing, that the kids just couldn't react. Within seconds, the man's body was covered with dense, wiry hair, but he also swelled up like some kind of muscle-bound balloon. The legs of his pants ripped as his thighs grew — the same with the arms of his sleeves as his biceps bulged.

By the time he turned around, the kids were looking at a huge, snarling werewolf with dripping fangs.

"I don't think he was telling us the tru—" Theo started to say, but before he finished his sentence, the werewolf leapt on him.

In a blink, the beast had Theo trapped on the floor, its jaws leaking saliva all over him.

David Michael Slater

Theo screamed. He was about to get his face ripped off. Max and Maddie screamed, too.

"STOP IT! STOP IT RIGHT NOW!"

Everyone turned to the door — even the werewolf — to see Delphine in her mermaid costume standing there, white as a sheet. Then, in a blur, she whipped the baby off her back and handed him to Maddie. Then she dove at the beast, knocking him off of Theo.

The kids were frozen yet again, shocked this time by the incredible sight of this beautiful woman having turned so violent and aggressive — more violent and aggressive than the werewolf. She wasn't growling and grunting, though. In fact, she was silent, silent but deadly, as she wrestled the beast into submission.

"The ropes!" she finally cried when the beast was pinned. "And close the curtains!"

Maddie ran to close the curtains while Max scrambled to hand Delphine the scraps of ropes lying at the foot of the chair. After a brief struggle, she had the werewolf sitting in it again with his hands tied behind his back. She reached into the bedside drawer behind them and took a sleep mask out, which she put over his eyes. Then she put her hands on either side of his head and whispered into his ear for a while. He slowly settled down.

But Delphine's hair was out of place from all her exertions, and one of *her* ears was exposed. And all three Mattigans — Theo, now sitting on the floor; Max, standing where he was; and Maddie, holding the baby — saw very clearly what was tucked behind it.

A gill.

When the werewolf went quiet, Delphine moved over and sat on the bed, exhausted. *"He should be okay now,"* she sighed, rearranging her hair.

Maddie peeked into the baby's shark costume. She was not surprised to see a real fin tucked up inside the fake one. "You're the Vancouver Island mermaid," she told the beautiful, but now terrifying woman. "I guess your legs change to fins in the water."

"I am and they do," Delphine admitted, taking this discovery in stride. "And you're the daughter of Layla Mattigan."

"I am."

"I thought I recognized you. You look just like her."

CHAPTER TEN

DIRECTLY RELATED

Delphine took the shark-baby back from Maddie and sat on the bed. "I apologize for my husband," she said, "but he cannot be held responsible for his actions in this condition, at least during the *change*. He *was* properly restrained. I'm sorry, but it was entirely your fault for breaking into my room and freeing him."

"Your *husband?*" Maddie gasped.

"He totally lied to us," Max complained. "He said he was robbed and thrown in here."

"And he tried to eat my face!" Theo complained, finally getting up from the floor.

"He is normally in control of whether he wishes to appear as a man or a werewolf," Delphine explained, "but not on full moons. On such nights, he agrees to be restrained. I expect you found him just before the moon took full effect, when he still looked human, but spoke more like a fox. He simply can't be trusted in that state. *Now,*" she said, clearly leaving the subject behind, "tell me what you know."

"We know that you're a mermaid married to a werewolf raising a shark-baby at an orphanage," Max said.

"Did you adopt it?" Maddie asked, the wheels in her mind suddenly turning.

The mermaid did not answer.

"I mean, I'm no expert in monsters, of course, but I'm thinking mermaid plus werewolf does not equal shark-baby."

"So, where'd you get it?" Max asked.

Maddie and Max looked at each other, realizing that they were asking the right questions even if they weren't getting answers.

"You were secretly raising him in your orphanage," Maddie said, thinking out loud. "But you told Theo you've been taking care of orphans for many years."

"Which means probably the shark-baby isn't the first baby monster you've adopted," Max said, turning to Delphine. "Maybe you've had lots. Maybe *all* of them."

"I bet," Maddie said, her face lighting up with the flush of discovery, "that the monsters somehow come to you — when they're babies — and when they're ready, you send them off to wherever you decide they will be safe to grow up."

"That is all correct," Delphine said. "You are very unusual kids,"

"True story!" Theo confirmed, even though he hadn't helped figure it all out.

"And the shark-baby sighting?" Max asked. "Are you really hiding just because too many people were coming around your orphanage?"

"That is also correct," Delphine confirmed. "It was just an ordinary reporter doing an ordinary story on our orphanage, which is, for most of our children, perfectly ordinary. Someone left the wrong door open."

"So, what does our mom have to do with all this?" Max asked.

"Your mother discovered how we come to adopt the 'monsters,' as you call them."

"She was a physicist," Max pointed out. "I hardly think—"

"Her discovery of our operation was not intentional."

"Then where in the world is she?"

"I can't possibly tell you that."

"Why not!" all three Mattigans demanded.

"Because she's no longer *in* the world."

"She's DEAD?" the kids screamed, wobbling on their feet.

Delphine held up her hands as if to catch them all. "I'm sorry," she said. "I spoke without thinking. Your mother is perfectly alive — at least as far as I know." Then, seeing the confusion on the kids' faces, she added, "You mother did not come to Vancouver Island looking for monsters, of course. She came to prove that the Multiverse Theory is correct. Only, it turns out that the two are directly related."

"The multi-*what?*" Max asked, trying not to pass out.

"The theory that there are many universes full of countless worlds."

"She proved that there's more than one world?" Maddie asked, relieved, astounded, and amazed, all at the same time. "How did she do that?"

"By actually leaving this one."

CHAPTER ELEVEN

THE GUARDIAN

The Mattigan kids looked at each other. They weren't going to fall apart anymore, but they all felt the weight of this incredible news settling on them. It was just too much to take standing up, so they all sat down on the floor.

"*Multiverse,*" Max said, letting the word sink in. "*That* was her big project. Multiple universes!" He could hardly believe it — even after all they'd discovered. Finally, he looked up and said, "But, she told my dad it was a big surprise for him, especially."

"He doesn't want to know that monsters exist," Maddie added, "and I'm sure she knew that."

"The monsters," Delphine told the kids, "are delivered to us from across the Multiverse as infants. They are the very last of their kinds, the rarest creatures in all the worlds of all the universes — the most endangered and precious. They are brought to this world, this Earth, to be kept safe, because this tiny planet is not on any known maps. It is a speck too small and insignificant to attract attention, and so the perfect place to hide."

"I — we don't understand," Maddie said, speaking for herself and her brothers. "What's that got to do with our dad?"

"My husband and I were the first infants to be rescued. We were raised by the creature who brought us here, a citizen from another world, one who looked very much like those of this one: our guardian. When we became adults, he began bringing us other infants, so we could raise them as he did us."

"But—" Maddie said again. "We still don't see..."

"This went on for hundreds of years, and creatures of all sorts were brought here for safekeeping. But there was a time when our guardian thought his job was done. He returned and hoped to live out his life on this world."

"But..."

"He even took a wife."

"But…"

"And they had a child. But duty returned him to his calling. The creatures he thought safe were endangered again, and he was forced to leave his family."

"I'm totally lost here," Maddie sighed.

"Grandpa, Maddie," Max said. "She's talking about *Grandpa Joe. He* was the one rescuing monsters for hundreds of years. He retired and married Grandma, and they had Dad. But he left them to go back to his job. He's not even human. That's why Grandma didn't hate him so much for leaving them. *He's* the guardian. Mom must have found out he was involved with all this up here. She was going to tell Dad."

"Your grandfather saved many lives over these many centuries," Delphine said as her latest incredible news settled over the Mattigans. "But he was getting old and thinking of retiring when your mother discovered us here. The timing was perfect. It was a very difficult choice for her to make, knowing she could not say goodbye to her family, but her help was needed immediately, and there was simply no time. Layla Mattigan is now the guardian, out there in the Multiverse, searching for more precious lives for us to protect. It was she who brought us the shark-baby."

With no hesitation, Max, Maddie, and Theo Mattigan jumped back to their feet and shouted, in one voice, "Liar!"

The expression on Delphine's beautiful face was one of genuine surprise. "She wept over the decision, I assure you," she promised. "But like your grandfather, she—"

"She would *never* do that to our dad!" Maddie roared. "She would never do that to *us!* Not in a billion-trillion years and not in a gazillion universes!" She was ready to fight again.

"You're telling us *some* of the truth, so we'll believe a lie slipped in with it," Max declared. "Our dad taught us that trick."

"Where's our mom?" Theo demanded.

Delphine looked at the kids one at a time. She seemed to be considering something. Then she leaned over to her husband and whispered something into his ear again. When she straightened up, she was holding the rope she'd used to tie his hands behind his back.

This time, the werewolf didn't pounce, but he moved swiftly again. And again toward Theo. Before the littlest Mattigan could react, the beast had its claws around his throat.

"You are correct once again," Delphine admitted. "Your mother would have shared her discovery with the people of this world. We could not risk her exposing what we do here. Your kind would surely hunt down and kill our precious babies, so we forced her out into the Multiverse, where she is surely lost forever. It was unfortunate, but it was our only choice." Then she added, though not hopefully, "If there's any justice in the worlds, you'll find her now that you're going out there, too."

CHAPTER TWELVE

QUITE LITERALLY NOTHING

"Let's go," Delphine said to her husband, who seemed barely in control of himself. He was drooling and snarling. Then, to Max and Maddie, who were frozen in fear for their brother, she said, "If you call any attention to us, or try to run, Wolfie will eat your brother's face. Do you understand?"

"Yes," Max and Maddie both croaked.

All Theo could manage was a squeak.

"Go to the elevators," Delphine ordered.

The Mattigans did as they were told.

Maddie and Max stared at each other all the way down to the lobby, both thinking there was no way a werewolf was going to simply walk past the front desk of the hotel without calling attention to itself. But then the doors opened and they saw Harry Potter, Snow White, and Frankenstein waiting to get on.

No one looked twice at them as they were marched right out onto the beach, which was full of monsters dancing in the moonlight around torches stuck in the sand. There were even werewolves out there, and plenty of mermaids, too.

Delphine and Wolfie led the kids down the beach, which gave the kids renewed hope of getting noticed, but it turned out that the costume party wasn't just at their hotel. It was at *all* of the hotels. It was as if some big island holiday was being celebrated. When they reached the beach in front of the next one, it was just the same. Creatures of all sorts were dancing or playing volley-ball or sitting around bonfires roasting marshmallows. Someone yelled, "Awesome costume!" at Wolfie when they went past. "Don't get shot!"

Delphine and Wolfie exchanged a worried look at this, but didn't say anything. And neither said a word as they herded the kids further down the beach, past one

hotel after another. It was nearly nine o'clock, but still quite bright out.

As they walked, Max and Maddie exchanged more worried looks of their own, but neither could think of anything to do that wouldn't get their brother mauled. The best they could do was bug their eyes out at costumed monsters they passed along the way.

But all the passing partiers did was bug their eyes back out at them and smile.

Finally, after almost twenty minutes of trudging over the sand, the little group reached both the end of the beach and the start of the forest that surrounded all of the resorts.

"Can we talk about this?" Max asked before they were forced into the woods. "We Mattigans are incredibly good at keeping secrets."

"True story," Theo dared to add.

"Keep moving," Delphine said.

Wolfie grunted and shoved Theo forward, in past the first few trees. There was a path there, and quickly enough they were on it.

No one was around now, so Max felt safe to keep talking. "I'm totally serious," he promised. "We're probably the best secret-keepers in the world. In all the worlds. I mean, you don't even realize that we found—"

"Silence!" Delphine demanded.

So, they all walked on in silence. After a few minutes, they left the path and cut their own trail through the trees. Eventually, they stopped in front of a very large rock — a boulder, really.

Wolfie let go of Theo, but Delphine quickly grabbed him. Then the werewolf squatted down and heaved the huge rock over on its side.

Underneath was a hole hollowed out of the forest floor.

But it was not a hole filled with dirt and roots and bugs.

What was inside this hole was quite literally *nothing*.

CHAPTER THIRTEEN

GAME OVER

The empty space under the rock was dark, but not just dark — it was darker than dark, like a black hole. It was a swirling, cold sort of darkness that all three of the Mattigan kids knew at once was space that wasn't just... space.

Not one of them doubted that this was the way to other worlds.

To the Multiverse.

"We found Bigfoot first," Max said, talking fast, the way his sister had when she'd told their dad about booking this foolish trip. "Well, actually, he sort of found us, but — same difference. And we hid him in our basement, no problem. Well, it was a little bit of a problem, but that's not important right now. What's important is that we didn't tell a soul, not even our own father. That's why I'm saying we can keep secrets. You could totally trust us to—"

"What?" Delphine asked. She'd been momentarily distracted, looking into the darkness of the way between the worlds, but now she was looking at Max with curiosity — and concern.

"Yeah," he said, encouraged to finally have Delphine's full attention. "Then we found J-Rod, the alien. Funny story. He was in Vegas, hiding at the — another costume party, actually. Sort of. Doesn't matter. He came to our house, too — and was really thankful. After that, we went to New Orleans and found Dracula. And then Shady, the ghost — sort of ghost, I guess. We're actually not really sure what she—"

"Impossible!" Delphine snapped. "Now, *you* are lying. Wolfie, put them through." She shoved Theo over to the werewolf, who picked him up, holding him right over his head.

"Humpf on yumpf!" Theo cried out, squirming desperately. "Let me go!"

"Please, no!" Maddie begged, reaching her arms out to her brother, but afraid to move.

"I'm telling you the truth!" Max promised Delphine. "Your babies! They live with us now! They wouldn't want you do this! If we're gone, they are going to get found out!"

Wolfie had Theo held out over the edge now. He was ready to drop him into the hole. Into the Multiverse.

"Ridiculous," Delphine scoffed. "My babies are scattered to the winds, as we intended. I have not seen them since—"

"He is telling the truth, Mother," a calm, but firm voice said from behind the little group.

Everyone turned around.

There, standing with tears in his eyes, was the alien from another universe, raising a four-fingered hand in greeting. Alongside J-Rod stood three other creatures from worlds of their own, worlds they didn't remember: Bigfoot, Dracula, and Shade.

"Hello, Mattigans," J-Rod said. "Thought it might be a good time for the MBI to meet again."

Wolfie grunted joyfully and dropped Theo on the edge of the hole. Then, spraying slobber like a broken sprinkler, he ran to hug the monsters.

The littlest Mattigan spun his arms frantically, trying not to fall into the hole. Max and Maddie leapt over and each managed to grab a hand just before their brother was lost forever.

Delphine, with tears in her own eyes, looked at her children. Then she, too, walked over and hugged them, one at a time. "My babies," she said when Bigfoot let her go. But then she turned back to the kids and said, sounding angry, "But, they are together!"

"Told ya," Theo told her.

"You guys can join us," Max offered. "Shark-baby, too, when he's ready. If he can live on land like you can, which he obviously can. *What?*"

Delphine looked horrified.

"It's okay," J-Rod promised. "With Shady here, the travel was easy. She jumped right into the customs officer and—"

"No, you don't understand! None of you understand!"

Just then, something flew out of the hole and lodged itself in the tree the group was standing near.

It took a moment for everyone to see that it was a grappling hook.

And that it was attached to a rope.

Which was still hanging down into the hole.

Everyone rushed to the edge and looked into it.

Blackness.

The rope shook, and a moment later, they could hear the sounds of someone grunting with physical effort. A dim light broke the darkness. Then a helmet with a light on top emerged.

A face tilted up from under the helmet. Large goggles covered most of it, and the rest was in shadow. The face tilted down again as its owner clambered up and out of the hole.

The climber looked around at the rather large audience standing there in the woods, humans and monsters

alike, and then took the helmet off, revealing an unruly head of snow-white hair with a matching, and equally unruly, mustache and beard. They belonged to an old man with eyes that looked as if they'd seen just about all there was to see. He was old, but looked wily and wise.

"Grandpa Joe?" Maddie asked.

"What's going on?" the man asked Delphine. "Why is the channel open? I came to leave a message under the boulder. Who are these children?"

"These are your grandchildren, Joe," Delphine told him. "They've discovered everything. On their own. And they've found some of our babies." She pointed at J-Rod, Dracula, Bigfoot, and Shade, who had remained quietly watching the scene. They waved.

"Grandpa Joe?" Maddie asked again.

The kids' grandfather took a good look at them. "Chips off the old block, eh?" he asked. "Good job."

"Told ya," Theo said.

"You have a message for us?" Delphine asked. "Is it about a new infant?"

"No," Joe replied. "We need to evacuate — everyone. Incredibly, you seem to have already started the process. These folks being here is a great stroke of luck," he added, gesturing toward the monsters. "We can begin immediately."

"What do you mean *evacuate?*" Delphine asked, going pale.

"Earth has been discovered," Joe told her. "I'm not sure how, but I always knew this day might come."

"But—" was all Delphine could manage.

"We're finished," Joe said. "Everything we've accomplished here. It's done. Game *over.*"

CHAPTER FOURTEEN

LAYLA

At that moment, another grappling hook flew out of the hole. There was a loud *clang!* as it caught onto the first.

"Stand back!" Grandpa Joe shouted, forcing everyone away from the rim. "Get ready to run!"

Another light emerged from the depths, and then another helmet. Then another climber scrambled up onto the forest floor. When the helmet and goggles were removed this time, long red curls fell down around their owner's face.

And when the climber took her goggles off, the Mattigan kids, as they so often did, shared one voice. But this time it came out in an explosion of pure joy:

"Mommy!"

And then there were more tears — *lots* more tears. And lots more hugging.

"Mommy!" Theo cried, hugging her side. Then he said it again. And again. "Mommy! Mommy! Mommy!"

"We missed you so much!" Maddie managed, choking up.

Max got his hugs in, too, but he couldn't speak. Not a single word.

"Enough," Grandpa Joe said, and when the Mattigans didn't hear him over their happy blubbering, he said it again: "Enough!"

They all turned to him.

It was only now that Layla took in the rest of the crowd around the hole. She narrowed her eyes at the mermaid, then at the snarling werewolf, and then she finally seemed to understand that some sort of situation was at hand. She looked unsure of what to make of the other monsters standing around, watching with confused but friendly expressions.

"Don't bother sending me back through," she told Delphine. "I can find my way back now."

"How is it that you were in the Multiverse?" Grandpa Joe asked her.

"We forced her through the portal," Delphine explained. Now, she looked like the one ready to fall apart. "She discovered us before her children did. Two years ago, now. We're sorry we never told you."

When Grandpa Joe looked to Layla to confirm this, she nodded. "My research on the Multiverse," she said, "led me to identify what I thought was a nexus — this portal — here on the island. But before I scheduled my trip here, I had my team do extensive research on the island — they investigated past and present residents, businesses, and even travel records."

"And you found my name," Grandpa Joe guessed.

"Yes. And evidence that you purchased the Vancouver Island Beach Hotel — though I'm guessing you changed your name because Joe Mattigan vanishes from the records shortly afterward — all records."

Grandpa Joe nodded this time, but then looked at Delphine. "Well, I think it's clear how we were discovered." He looked back at Layla and said, "I presume you did not take precautions to make sure you weren't followed."

"Followed?" Layla asked, sounding furious. "Those two cost me two years of my life!" She was pointing to Delphine and Wolfie. "I spent those two years trying to find my way back. I talked to thousands of creatures in hundreds of worlds looking for help. But not one had ever heard of Earth. The only reason I finally found it is because — since you seemed to have disappeared here — on a whim, I also starting asking if anyone had ever heard of Joe Mattigan. It seems *everyone* knows Joe Mattigan. It only took a few months to track you down. So, no, I wasn't worried about being followed. *I've* been following *you!*"

CHAPTER FIFTEEN

CORNERED AND ALONE

"Well," Grandpa Joe said, looking grave, "someone you spoke to along the way was the wrong someone, and now an even wronger someone is on the way here."

"And the children have made it worse," Delphine said, "by bringing these creatures together under one roof."

"Fools!" Joe sighed. "But no matter — I'll take them out now."

"Please, Grandpa Joe," Maddie begged, "can you tell us what's going on?" She'd listened to the adults' exchange with intense interest, but she felt as confused as she was amazed.

"The Collector," Joe said. "He knows about Earth

now. He's on his way. We have no choice but to evacuate."

"The Collector?" The way Joe had said the name gave Maddie that sick feeling in her stomach that she got when she lied.

"Oh, no," Layla said, her hand going to her mouth.

"They don't know," Delphine said, waving at the kids. Then she turned to them and said, "The Collector is the richest, most powerful citizen in the Multiverse. He is also the cruelest. He prowls the worlds, searching for the rarest of all creatures. He hunts them down and freezes them — turns them into statues — for his collection. It is from him that we have been hiding your friends."

"No one's statue-ing my monsters!" Theo shouted. He started to run to them, but J-Rod held up a four-fingered hand that stopped him. He called Dracula, Bigfoot, and Shade over, and they exchanged a few quick words.

When they were done conferring, J-Rod stepped forward and addressed Delphine and Grandpa Joe. "We are very grateful for all you have done for us," he said. "But we will stay here. This is where we live."

"The Collector will find you," Joe told them, and not kindly. "He will freeze you solid. And you will end up on display in his palace. Is that what you want?"

Dracula stepped forward. "Excuse me," he said. "But haz zis Collector found hiz prey in a group before? Or does he catch zem cornered and alone?"

"Well, alone, I'd assume," Joe granted.

"Ve vill vait for him, zen," Dracula declared. "Ve vill verk together to defend our home."

Before Grandpa Joe could respond to this, everyone heard the sounds of movement in the woods.

Wolfie immediately rolled the boulder back over the hole between the worlds. Then he leapt on top of it and unleashed a wicked howl to warn the intruders away.

"Darling, no!" Delphine cried, but no sooner had she done so than a cracking bang sent everyone diving to the forest floor.

"Gunshot!" Joe shouted. Wolfie leapt from the boulder, unharmed, and bolted into the woods. Two figures in camouflage could be seen running in the direction he'd gone.

Everyone got up, shaken.

"They will never catch him," Delphine assured the worried group. "He will meet us back at the hotel tomorrow morning." But then she added, "When he returns, we must all have a serious talk, for one thing is certain: Hunters or not, this world is no longer safe for our kind."

CHAPTER SIXTEEN

REUNION

At ten o'clock, the Mattigan kids were sitting on a bed in Marcus and Max's room, trying to help Max talk. But no matter what they did, he just couldn't make a sound come out of his mouth.

"I think you're in shock," Maddie concluded.

Max nodded. He'd never been so embarrassed in all his life. He'd never been so happy, either.

"It'll pass," Maddie promised. "Let's watch TV until Dad gets here."

Max nodded again, so Maddie grabbed the remote and clicked the set on.

"Dad, ho!" Theo shouted, pointing at the screen.

"Hello, I'm Marcus Mattigan," their father told them.

"If that's his real name," Theo said, since his brother wasn't able to. Max smiled at him, weakly.

"You may know me as the host of *Monstrous Lies with Marcus Mattigan*," their dad continued. He was standing in an official-looking office. "I'm here on behalf of the Vancouver Island Tourism Department to ask you to please not put anyone's life at risk by firing weapons at imaginary werewolves. If it's not enough that there are no such things as werewolves — or monsters of any sort, of course — I'd like to inform you that the source of this million-dollar reward for the werewolf's pelt is *totally bogus*. The man who offered the reward cannot pay it. He is *completely broke*. So, please, enjoy the island while you are here, and let everyone else do the same. Thank you."

The kids looked at each other, unsure of what to say about this. There was really nothing to say. It didn't matter anyway, because a moment later Marcus opened the door.

All three kids jumped off the bed as if it had been electrified.

"Everything all right?" he asked.

"Better than alright," Maddie said. "Mostly."

"Interested. How's that?"

"It's sort of hard to know where to start. There's kind of a lot."

"Hooked. Let's start with door number one."

"Okay," Maddie said. "Since you asked."

The kids led their baffled father to the door to Maddie and Theo's adjoining room, which was closed.

"There's a surprise for you in there," Maddie told him. "A really, really big one. We'll be waiting for you to come back in here when you're done. Just go on in."

"This," Marcus said, "is very strange."

"You have no idea."

"Is what I'm saying."

"Trust us."

"I do."

Marcus opened the door and went through.

Maddie carefully closed it behind him, but then all three kids pressed their ears up against its smooth, cool surface.

They heard a gasp and the sound of their parents crying out each other's names. But then, out of politeness, they backed away.

Thirty minutes later, Marcus and Layla came into the room holding hands. The kids jumped off the bed again, wanting desperately to learn how the reunion had gone.

"I — I don't know what to say," Marcus said. He looked totally transformed. He was beaming. His crazy Mattigan hair seemed even crazier than normal, like it was as excited as he was. "She says she can't explain where she's been yet," he said, sounding dazed and confused, but accepting. "Not until I visit two other rooms. How can this get any stranger? I feel like I'm in some alternate world."

"You have no idea," Maddie said.

"Trust us," Theo told him.

"I do."

"Told ya."

This time, Max, Maddie, and Theo took their father into the hall. They led him to a room just a few doors down.

"We'll be waiting for you," Maddie said.

After another thirty minutes, the door to their room opened again. Marcus came in alone. "Speechless," he said. "Flabbergasted. I don't understand what's happening, or why or how. And I don't care right now. I'm so angry at my father and so happy to have him back. I've never been so confused or so happy in my life. But he told me the most ridiculous story I've ever heard, and my life is all about hearing ridiculous stories. The man is certifiably insane. We're going to have to find him professional help."

"Hold on, Dad," Maddie said.

"What now?"

"Well, I know you've told us about fifty times you wouldn't want to know if—"

"At this point, I'm game for anything. I don't think I'm capable of being surprised."

"Well, then," Maddie said, "there's one more room."

The kids led their dad to another door. This time, they went in ahead of him. Marcus followed them in, shaking his head as if he were still trying to see through the fog on the deck of the ferry that had brought him to this fantasy island. His wife and father came in behind him.

Marcus froze.

Sitting in chairs and on the beds were an alien, a Sasquatch, a vampire, and a sable ghost. There was also a werewolf next to a woman with a baby in her arms — a baby with a shark fin on its back.

Slowly, respectfully, the monsters stood up and bowed.

"Greetings," J-Rod said, once again holding up a four-fingered hand.

Marcus Mattigan, professional skeptic and star of the hit show *Monstrous Lies with Marcus Mattigan*, fainted where he stood.

"He's in shock," Max said, his voice finally back. "It'll pass."

POSTSCRIPT:

WEREWOLF!

And that, dear readers, is the story of how the Mattigan family *finally* got back together — and how none of them got their faces eaten. (I'm going to assume that goes for you, as well, since you are still reading this. Congratulations!)

Max, Maddie, and Theo had to go to the ends of the Earth — literally, the *end* of the Earth — to solve all of the mysteries in their very mysterious lives. But as you know very well by now, that's the kind of kids they are.

But now their troubles *really* begin.

Because, as you know, The Collector is coming.

The good news is that the Mattigans will face the challenge as a family — a complete family.

Maybe *that's* what we're all searching for: whatever completes us.

Discuss among yourselves.

How's *your* search going, by the way? (I didn't forget.)

Not sure what completes you yet?

Well, here's some advice that might help you search for your search: Keep your portals boulder-free — and always open the curtains *before* you rescue anyone tied to a chair.

Sincerely,

Your pal

About The Author

David Michael Slater writes shockingly good books for children, teens, and adults. He promises that he doesn't use a ghostwriter. You can learn more about David and the work he really wrote, all by his living self, at www.davidmichaelslater.com.

COMING TO A BASEMENT NEAR YOU

About Mysterious Monsters

Mysterious Monsters is a humorous six-book early chapter book series full of mystery and adventure. When Marcus Mattigan, star of the popular show "Monstrous Lies with Marcus Mattigan" offers to let his kids, Maddie, Max, and Theo, travel around the country with him as he exposes frauds and fakes, the trio manages to find and capture the world's most mysterious and elusive creatures — and then to hide them in their increasingly crowded basement. As you can imagine, with each book, the situation gets more and more hairy.

Credits

This book is a work of art produced by
Incorgnito Publishing Press.

Susan Comninos
Editor

Mauro Sorghienti
Illustrator/Artist

Star Foos
Designer

Janice Bini
Chief Reader

Daria Lacy
Graphic Production

Michael Conant
Publisher

January 2019
Incorgnito Publishing Press

Books in this Series:

Book One - **BIGFOOT**

Book Two - **ALIEN**

Book Three - **VAMPIRE**

Book Four - **GHOST**

Book Five - **WEREWOLF**

Book Six - **THE COLLECTOR** (Fall 2019)